Hispanic Headliners

Sonia Sotomayor

Supreme Court Justice

Zella Williams

PowerKiDS press
New York

Published in 2011 by The Rosen Publishing Group, Inc.
29 East 21st Street, New York, NY 10010

First Edition

Editor: Joanne Randolph
Book Design: Kate Laczynski
Photo Researcher: Jessica Gerweck

Photo Credits: Cover, p. 1 Scott Applewhite/AFP/Getty Images; p. 4–5 Jewel Samad/AFP/Getty Images; pp. 6–8 The White House via Getty Images; p. 9 Shutterstock.com; pp. 10–11, 14–15 Alex Wong/Getty Image News/Getty Images; p. 12 Doug Collier/AFP/Getty Images; pp. 13, 21 © Associated Press/AP Images; p. 16 Paul J. Richards/AFP/Getty Images; pp. 17 (top), 22 Mark Wilson/Getty Images; p. 17 (bottom) © www.iStockphoto.com/Greg Panosian; p. 18 Jared Wickerham/Getty Images; p. 19 Abby Brack/Getty Images.

Library of Congress Cataloging-in-Publication Data

Williams, Zella.
   Sonia Sotomayor : Supreme Court justice / Zella Williams. — 1st ed.
      p. cm. — (Hispanic headliners)
   Includes index.
   ISBN 978-1-4488-1455-8 (library binding) — ISBN 978-1-4488-1474-9 (pbk.) —
ISBN 978-1-4488-1475-6 (6-pack)
   1. Sotomayor, Sonia, 1954—Juvenile literature. 2. Hispanic American judges—Biography—Juvenile literature. 3. Judges—United States-Biography—Juvenile literature. I. Title.
   KF8745.S67W55 2011
   347.73'2634-dc22
   [B]

Manufactured in the United States of America

CPSIA Compliance Information: Batch #WS10PK: For Further Information contact Rosen Publishing, New York, New York at 1-800-237-9932

CONTENTS

What if someone told you that you were about to become a **Supreme Court justice**? What if he or she also told you that you would be the third

President Barack Obama claps for new associate Supreme Court justice, Sonia Sotomayor.

woman and first
Hispanic person to
hold that office?
Someone gave Sonia
Sotomayor just
such news in 2009.
Getting to this
point was not easy,
though. She had to
work hard.

Sonia Sotomayor was born in the Bronx, New York, on June 25, 1954. Her parents, Juan and Celina Baez Sotomayor, were born in Puerto Rico.

Here a young Sonia is pictured with her mother and father, Celina and Juan.

Sonia Sotomayor is six or seven years old here.

Juan Sotomayor worked as a toolmaker. Celina worked as a nurse. Sonia's father spoke only Spanish, so she grew up in a bilingual household.

Sonia and her mother have stayed close through the years.

After Juan Sotomayor's death, Celina raised Sonia and her brother, Juan, on her own. Sonia worked hard at her studies. She graduated from Cardinal Spellman High

Sonia Sotomayor is shown here at her eighth grade graduation.

Sotomayor went to Princeton University, shown here.

School as the **valedictorian** in 1972. She studied history at Princeton University. She then received her law degree from Yale Law School in 1979.

After earning her law degree, Sonia Sotomayor took a job as assistant district attorney in New York City. In this job, she **prosecuted** people who had committed small crimes and

Working in private practice was a big change for Sotomayor. She worked for a firm called Pavia and Harcourt.

people who had hurt and killed others. In 1984, she left the district attorney's office and spent eight years in private practice.

In 1992, Sonia Sotomayor became a judge of the Federal District Court for the Southern District of New York. It was her job to listen to and make decisions on cases

George Steinbrenner, an owner of the Yankees, is shown talking about the baseball strike in 1994.

Here Sotomayor stands in her office when she was a federal court judge.

presented by lawyers. She is remembered most for a decision she made in 1995. This decision ended a 232-day Major League Baseball strike.

What was the next stop in Sonia Sotomayor's promising career? She became a judge of the U.S. Court of **Appeals** for the Second Circuit in 1998. She heard appeals on more than

Sonia Sotomayor worked hard in her job as a judge for the U.S. Court of Appeals.

3,000 cases and wrote nearly 400 majority opinions. A majority opinion is one on which most members of that court agree.

In May 2009, Sonia Sotomayor was **nominated** by President Barack Obama to fill a seat on the Supreme Court. As an associate justice on this court,

Sotomayor was sworn in as a Supreme Court justice in August 2009. Her mother held the Bible.

Sonia Sotomayor stands with associate justices Antonin Scalia (left) and Clarence Thomas (right).

it would be her job to make sure decisions by lower courts upheld the **Constitution**. She was approved as associate Supreme Court justice in August 2009.

This is the U.S. Supreme Court building, in Washington, D.C.

Sonia Sotomayor has done more than just hear cases. In 1976, she married Kevin Noonan. However, after about six years their marriage ended. She worked as an

Sotomayor is a baseball fan. She takes the mound with New York Yankee Jorge Posada here.

Sotomayor and actor Esai Morales are at a National Hispanic Foundation for the Arts event.

adjunct, or part-time, professor at New York University from 1998 to 2007. She also began teaching law students at Columbia University in 1999.

Sonia Sotomayor has always worked hard to do well. In 1976, while she was in college, she won the Pyne Prize because of that work. She has **honorary degrees** from many colleges

Sotomayor speaks at an event held in her honor by the U.S. Court of Appeals judges in 2009.

and universities, including Princeton and Lehman College. Sotomayor has also won awards for her hard work as a Latina professional.

As a justice of the Supreme Court, Sotomayor has a job that most judges only dream about. What will happen in the years to come? Only time will

tell. We can hope that she judges cases fairly and upholds the U.S. Constitution. It is a big job, but Sonia Sotomayor has shown that she is not afraid to work hard.

GLOSSARY

appeals (uh-PEELZ) Asking judges in higher courts to take a second look at legal decisions.

Constitution (kon-stih-TOO-shun) The basic rules by which the United States is governed.

honorary degrees (AH-neh-rer-ree duh-GREEZ) Ranks or titles given by colleges or universities to honor, or recognize, people for what they have done.

justice (JUS-tis) Another word for a judge.

nominated (NAH-muh-nayt-ed) Suggested for an award or a position.

prosecuted (PRAH-sih-kyoot-ed) Took legal action against someone for the purpose of punishment.

Supreme Court (suh-PREEM KORT) The highest court in the United States.

valedictorian (va-luh-dik-TOR-ee-un) The student with the highest grades and who generally gives a speech at graduation.

INDEX

A
assistant district
    attorney, 10

B
Bronx, New York, 6

C
Cardinal Spellman
    High School,
    8
Constitution, 17, 22

H
history, 9
household, 7

J
job, 10, 12, 17, 22

L
law degree, 9–10

N
nurse, 7

O
Obama, Barack, 16
office, 5, 11

P
Princeton University,
    9, 21

Puerto Rico, 6

S
Sotomayor, Celina
    Baez (mother), 6–8
Sotomayor, Juan
    (brother), 8
Sotomayor, Juan
    (father), 6–8

U
U.S. Court of Appeals,
    14

Y
Yale Law School, 9

WEB SITES

Due to the changing nature of Internet links, PowerKids Press has developed
an online list of Web sites related to the subject of this book. This site is
updated regularly. Please use this link to access the list:
www.powerkidslinks.com/hh/sotomayor/